When I Carried You in My Belly

by

Thrity Umrigar

Illustrated by Ziyue Chen

RP | KIDS

PHILADELPHIA

Published by Running Press Kids,
An Imprint of Perseus Books, LLC.,
A Subsidiary of Hachette Book Group, Inc.

Books published by Running Press are available at special discounts for bulk purchases
in the United States by corporations, institutions, and other organizations.
For more information, please contact the Special Markets Department at Perseus Books,
2300 Chestnut Street, Suite 200, Philadelphia, PA 19103, or call
(800) 810-4145, ext. 5000, or e-mail special.markets@perseusbooks.com.

ISBN 978-0-7624-6058-8

Library of Congress Control Number: 2016940459

9 8 7 6 5 4 3 2 1
Digit on the right indicates the number of this printing

Designed by Frances J. Soo Ping Chow
Edited by Marlo Scrimizzi
Typography: Devious and ITC Avante Garde Gothic

Running Press Book Publishers
2300 Chestnut Street
Philadelphia, PA 19103–4371

Visit us on the web!
www.runningpress.com/rpkids

To Judy
for what was

and Binu and Zoya
for what will be

When I carried you in my belly,
we went to a party once.

A little boy pointed at me and yelled,
"Mama, that lady ate all the food!"

"No, no, honey," his mama whispered.
"She has a baby in her belly."
The boy's eyes grew large.
"She ate a whole *baby*?"

I was laughing so hard
you began to laugh, too.

And that must be the reason why
you have the greatest laugh today.

When I carried you in my belly,
your daddy would kiss you there
and plan to play ball with you
as soon as you could walk.

And that is why you have become . . .

my fearless little sprite today.

When I carried you in my belly,
Grandpa baked a chocolate cake each week,
and cupcakes with frosting and sprinkles,
and lots of love inside.

And that is why you became . . .

the sweetest girl that I know.

When I carried you in my belly,
Nana built you a wooden crib.
She'd whistle while she polished it,
with her old and loving hands.

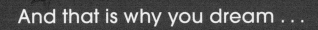

And that is why you dream . . .

the softest dreams at night.

When I carried you in my belly,
I sang to you all day.
In many different languages,
I sang you songs of joy.

And that is why you feel at home . . .

any place in the world.

When I carried you in my belly,
we danced every dance together:
the rumba and the samba,
the tango and the fandango.

And that is why your feet . . .

tap in rhythm to the earth today.

When I carried you in my belly,
we fed kittens out of saucers,
baked bread for our neighbors,
and hung bird feeders on the trees.

And that is why you have . . .

the biggest heart in the world.

When I carried you in my belly,
we stared at the nighttime sky.
We watched the stars a-twinkle
as we danced in the moonlight.

And that is why your eyes . . .

sparkle each time you smile.

When I carried you in my belly,
I talked to you all day.
I lay in the dark with you
and whispered all my dreams.

I felt your kicks and heartbeats
as clearly as my own.

And that is why, my baby,
now that I no longer carry you in my belly . . .

I carry you in my heart,
each day.